The Magic Bunny

Lucy Daniels

STORY ONE:
Easter Bunnies

CHAPTER ONE – Page 9

CHAPTER TWO – Page 23

CHAPTER THREE – Page 33

CHAPTER FOUR – Page 49

CHAPTER FIVE – Page 63

CHAPTER SIX – Page 77

STORY TWO:
The Talent Show

CHAPTER ONE – Page 95

CHAPTER TWO – Page 105

CHAPTER THREE – Page 121

CHAPTER FOUR – Page 135

CHAPTER FIVE – Page 145

CHAPTER SIX – Page 159

STORY ONE:
Easter Bunnies

CHAPTER ONE

"Breakfast time, Bertie!" Amelia said.

The Beagle puppy scrabbled at the bars of his cage, his eyes fixed on the bowl of food in Amelia's hand. When she opened the door, Bertie shot towards her, his tail wagging.

Amelia grinned as she set the bowl

down, and the little dog buried his face
in the food. Sam smiled from the sink,
where he was filling water bowls. It was
the Easter holidays, and they had both
come early to Animal Ark to give the
overnight patients their breakfast.

"I hope it stays sunny tomorrow!"
Amelia said, filling a sick tabby's bowl
with a special food to help it recover.

"Well, even if it's tipping it down, we'll be having the Easter egg hunt at my house," Sam said. "My dad's been planning it for weeks. It's the highlight of his year."

"It's going to be awesome!" Amelia said. "There are so many great hiding places in your garden, I can't wait."

Just then, Julia popped her head around the door. She was the receptionist at Animal Ark. "There's a friend of yours in reception," she said. "I thought you'd want to come and say hello."

Amelia and Sam quickly washed their hands and headed through to the waiting area.

11

"Izzy!" cried Sam.

Their classmate sat beside her mum with an animal carrier on her lap. Izzy's face looked pale under her straight black fringe, and she was biting her lip. But as she glanced up and saw Amelia and Sam, she managed a smile. *I hope her rabbits are OK,* Amelia thought.

"Is that Tulip?" Sam asked, nodding towards the animal carrier. Izzy's rabbit, Tulip, had once escaped from her back garden, and Sam and Amelia had helped to find her. Then, when they discovered that Tulip had run away because she'd been bored, they had surprised Izzy with a pair of new rabbits – Rose and

12

Poppy – to keep Tulip company.

"It's Rose," Izzy said.

"Is she sick?" Sam asked, anxiously.

Izzy didn't answer at once, and Amelia felt a 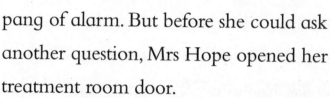 pang of alarm. But before she could ask another question, Mrs Hope opened her treatment room door.

"Izzy and Rose," she called. Then she added, "Sam and Amelia, why don't you come in too and give us a hand?"

Once they were all inside the treatment room, Izzy set her carrier down on the table. "Let's take a look at Rose, then,"

Mrs Hope said, putting on gloves.

Izzy put her hands into the carrier, but the rabbit growled and scrambled away from her.

"Hush, it's all right," Izzy said, scooping her bunny out. Rose growled again, and kicked, struggling in Izzy's grip. Sam and Amelia exchanged worried glances as Izzy passed her rabbit to the vet. *That's not like Rose at all!* thought Amelia.

Mrs Hope held the bunny firmly across  the shoulders with one hand while giving her long, calming strokes with the other.

Even so, Rose sat stiffly with her ears pressed back and her eyes wide and staring. The last time Amelia had seen Rose, she had been playful and had loved being held. But that wasn't the only thing that had changed. Amelia couldn't help noticing how much bigger Rose had grown. Just a few weeks ago, she'd been quite a small rabbit. Now she looked huge, with a big, round belly.

"I think something's wrong with Rose," Izzy told Mrs Hope. "She keeps growling at Poppy and Tulip, and she doesn't like being cuddled any more."

"And she's put on a lot of weight," Izzy's mum added.

As Mrs Hope kept stroking Rose,
the rabbit seemed to relax a little, her
ears pricking up slightly as she looked
about the room. Mrs Hope inspected the
rabbit's eyes and ears, then listened to
her heart and lungs with a stethoscope.
Finally, she felt all around Rose's tummy.
Rose's ears instantly flicked back again,
and she tried to squirm away, but the vet
held her in place until she'd finished her
examination.

"OK, Rose, we're all done," Mrs Hope
said, putting the bunny back into her
carrier. The vet smiled as she took off her
gloves, and Amelia noticed a twinkle in
her eye.

"Is Rose ill?" Izzy asked anxiously.

Mrs Hope shook her head, her smile broadening. "No. Not at all. Rose is very healthy. In fact … She's pregnant!" Izzy and her mum both gaped at Mrs Hope. Sam and Amelia exchanged a look of surprise. *Pregnant?*

"She can't be!" Sam said. "I mean – how is that possible? All Izzy's rabbits are girls."

Mrs Hope raised an eyebrow. "I'm afraid I'll have to disagree with you there," she said.

Izzy and her mum both stared at Rose in shocked silence.

"Well, we know Tulip's definitely a girl," Amelia reasoned. "You've examined her before. And clearly Rose is too!"

"So, Poppy must be the dad!" Sam said.

Mrs Hope nodded. "It is an easy mistake to make when rabbits are young." She turned to Izzy's mum. "If you bring Poppy in, I'll check him over. If he is a male rabbit, which really isn't in much doubt, he should have a very small operation to prevent any more pregnancies."

"But … what should we do with Rose?" Izzy asked. "Will she be OK?"

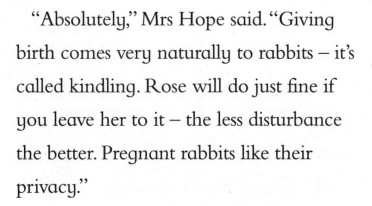

"Absolutely," Mrs Hope said. "Giving birth comes very naturally to rabbits – it's called kindling. Rose will do just fine if you leave her to it – the less disturbance the better. Pregnant rabbits like their privacy."

"Do we need to feed her anything special?" Izzy's mum asked.

"Just give her plenty of clean water and nutritious food," Mrs Hope said. "Maybe some leafy greens and alfalfa hay in addition to her normal pellets. And you'll need to make her a nesting box. When she's almost ready to give birth, she'll line it with hay and some of her own fur to make it safe and warm for her kits."

"Kits? Is that what baby rabbits are called?" Amelia asked.

"Yes, it's short for kittens," Mrs Hope said. Then she turned again to Izzy's mum. "You should probably get started on the nesting box right away – Rose is quite far along. I'd say she's likely to give birth any time in the next week."

Izzy stared open-mouthed at the vet.

"A week!" Izzy's mum gasped. "I mean – what a wonderful surprise. I'm very glad Rose isn't sick. But there's so much to do! I'll get started on her nesting box right away. And a new hutch for Poppy!"

"A second hutch is a great idea," Mrs Hope said. "You'll want to keep him away from the girl rabbits until he's had his operation. But don't worry about Rose and her babies. We'll give you all the advice and help you need."

Amelia squeezed her hands together, her excitement rising. Baby bunnies in less than a week! She caught Sam's eye and saw he was grinning.

"We'll help too!" Sam promised Izzy.

Amelia nodded. "Any way we can!"

CHAPTER TWO

The next day, after a busy morning hunting Easter eggs at Sam's house, Amelia and Sam went to fetch Poppy. The Hopes had agreed to let the bunny come to stay, even though Animal Ark wasn't officially open on Sundays. When they arrived at Izzy's house, Amelia could

hear the steady rasp of a saw coming from the back garden. The clean smell of sawdust mingled with the scent of the roses that climbed the weather-worn brickwork.

Sam had barely rapped the knocker when Izzy opened the door, her face glowing with excitement. "Mum's making Rose's nesting box!" she said. "And Rose has started pulling out her fur to make a nest. Mrs Hope said that rabbits only do that when they're almost ready to give birth. So I think the babies might come really soon!"

Amelia felt a thrill of excitement. "I've never seen baby bunnies in real life," she said, following Izzy inside. "But I've been watching videos online and they look so funny and cute – almost like teeny weeny hippos!"

"I've been watching videos too," Izzy said, leading them through the house. "It's actually made me quite nervous. Rose could have up to fourteen babies!"

"Whoa!" Sam said. "That is a lot of bunnies!"

When they reached the back garden,

they found Izzy's mum sawing at her workbench in front of the shed. She straightened up and pushed a strand of hair behind her ear. "Happy Easter!" she said. "Thank you for coming to fetch Poppy. We've got so much to do here, it's a real help. The nesting box and new hutch are coming along, but they won't be ready for a few days yet. Now we know that Poppy's a boy, we've been keeping him apart from the other two."

"He's in the rabbit run," Izzy said, sadly. "But he's not very happy. I think he's missing his friends."

An animal carrier sat ready in front of the run, where Poppy was nibbling at

the grass. In the hutch at the back of the garden, Amelia could see Tulip munching happily on a pile of salad leaves. Rose sat hunched in a corner, stiff and watchful. As Tulip hopped over to her, Rose growled and lunged, sending Tulip scrambling away with a startled squeak.

"Rose! Don't be such a grump!" Izzy said. She turned to Amelia and Sam

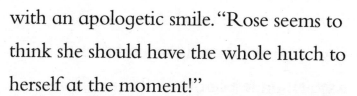

with an apologetic smile. "Rose seems to think she should have the whole hutch to herself at the moment!"

As Amelia watched Rose hunched in the corner, she remembered the internet research she'd done.

"Mrs Hope did say Rose would want more privacy now she's pregnant," Amelia said. "Maybe she *should* have the hutch to herself for a while. We're taking Poppy to the vet for his operation anyway. How about we take Tulip as well? I read that it's sensible for female rabbits to have an operation too, so there definitely won't be any more surprise baby bunnies!"

Izzy's mum nodded thoughtfully. "We'd been planning to get all the rabbits spayed anyway. I think that's a good idea."

"Rose will be much happier with a bit more space!" Izzy said, peering at the grumpy pregnant bunny. Rose was still sitting stiffly in the corner of the hutch

with her ears flicked back.

Amelia turned to Tulip and smiled. "Sorry, Tulip — it's time for you to take a trip to the vet!"

CHAPTER THREE

It was the last day of the Easter holidays. Amelia had spent the past few days with her dad, who lived in York. She'd had a great time – Dad had even taken her to visit a birds of prey centre – but Amelia was happy to be back at Animal Ark. She sat in the treatment room with

Poppy snuggled on her lap. As she stroked the rabbit's velvety ears, her eyes were fixed on the treatment table where Sam was holding Tulip belly-up for Mrs Hope.

The vet frowned slightly as she

 examined a small puckered line of stiches that ran across the rabbit's tummy. Poppy had already recovered from his operation, but Amelia knew that female rabbits took longer to heal, and there was a greater chance of infection.

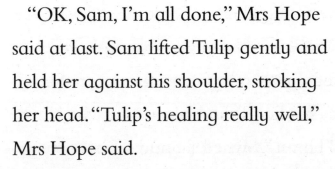

"OK, Sam, I'm all done," Mrs Hope said at last. Sam lifted Tulip gently and held her against his shoulder, stroking her head. "Tulip's healing really well," Mrs Hope said.

Amelia let her breath out in a sigh of relief.

"She'll need to stay here a few more days," continued the vet, "but she'll recover quickly, and will likely live a longer and healthier life now, too. Poppy's ready to go home anytime."

Amelia scratched Poppy behind his ears. "Did you hear that? You're ready to go home!"

"He'd just better hope that Rose

doesn't try and bite him!" Sam joked.

"Hasn't Izzy's mum finished the new hutch yet?" asked Amelia, concerned.

"Not quite," said Sam.

"Hmm," Mrs Hope said. "That doesn't sound ideal."

"There are lots of spare cages here in the animal hotel," Amelia said.

Mrs Hope sighed. "You're right. I think it might be best for Poppy to stay here until the hutch is ready."

"Julia will be happy!" Amelia said. "She's been playing with Poppy every chance she gets. I think she'll miss these two when they go home."

Once Tulip was safely back in her pen,

Sam and Amelia took Poppy through to reception.

"Ah! My favourite furry friend," Julia said, wheeling her chair away from her desk and reaching for the bunny, her eyes shining. Amelia passed Poppy into the receptionist's arms.

"I've got a special treat for you!" Julia told the rabbit. She wheeled back to her desk and offered Poppy a small piece of apple. Then 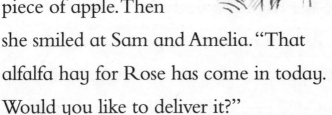 she smiled at Sam and Amelia. "That alfalfa hay for Rose has come in today. Would you like to deliver it?"

"We can check on Rose at the same time," Sam said, excitedly. "Maybe we'll even get to see her give birth!"

Heading through from the treatment room with a handful of papers, Mrs Hope stopped and shook her head. "Actually, it's better for Rose if everyone stays away from her as much as possible until after the kindling," she said, smiling kindly. "Right now, Rose needs peace and quiet and as little stress as possible. But once the kits are born, she'll be back to her old self quickly."

Amelia couldn't help feeling a little disappointed, but she and Sam both nodded and smiled. "We'll just drop the hay off and go," Amelia said. "We want what's best for Rose and the babies!"

"Aw, thanks for bringing this!" Izzy said, as Sam handed her the bag of hay. "I'll put some in Rose's hutch right now. Mum's out shopping, but she won't mind you two coming in. Do you want to see Rose's new nesting box?"

Amelia stepped back. "Actually, Mrs Hope said we should give Rose plenty of space until after the kindling."

"We don't want to make her feel stressed out," Sam said.

"Well, you can take a quick peek," said

Izzy. "Rose is all snuggled up inside. I don't think she'll even notice."

When they reached the sunny garden, Izzy led Sam and Amelia straight to Rose's hutch. Amelia could see a large wooden box inside it. Rose's furry black and white body filled half the box, and hay lined the bottom.

But as Amelia looked more closely, she saw something that made her heart skip a beat. Sam gasped, and Izzy let out a squeak of excitement.

Nestled up against Rose's tufty fur, four damp, wrinkly babies were squirming and nudging at Rose with their noses. Three of them were deep pink with just the faintest silvery sheen of fur, while the other one had black and pink patches. They all had tiny buds of ears folded back against their heads, and their eyes were closed tight. Their heads looked too

big for their funny little bodies, and, as they wiggled, they batted blindly at their mother with teeny, clumsy-looking paws. In the quiet, Amelia could hear little peeps and squeaks coming from them.

"Oh …" Amelia whispered. "Have you ever seen anything so cute?"

Blinking in astonishment, Izzy slowly shook her head. "They weren't there ten minutes ago!" she said. "They must have just been born!"

"They're so tiny," Sam breathed, his eyes fixed on the squirming kits. He frowned. "I hope they're OK. Maybe we should call Animal Ark?"

Izzy brought the house phone out into

the garden and tapped in the number.
Amelia and Sam listened eagerly as Izzy
spoke with the vet.

"Do we need to do anything for the
babies?" Sam asked, as soon as Izzy put
the phone down.

"Mrs Hope says that if
they are moving and
trying to feed, we should
just leave Rose to it."
Izzy looked down at
the tiny rabbits, her lips
pinched together in a
worried line. "But how
will we know for sure if
they're all right?"

"Maybe we should get them out and check them over?" Amelia asked.

Izzy shook her head. "Mrs Hope said not to hold them for the first few days unless absolutely necessary."

Amelia felt oddly relieved. The baby rabbits looked so fragile, with thin, almost translucent skin. It made her feel big and clumsy just watching them. She wasn't sure she would dare to pick one up, even if it was allowed.

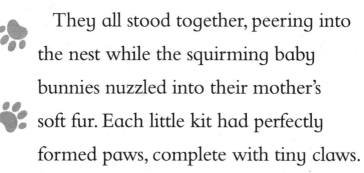

They all stood together, peering into the nest while the squirming baby bunnies nuzzled into their mother's soft fur. Each little kit had perfectly formed paws, complete with tiny claws.

The baby rabbits wriggled constantly, unlike their mum, who seemed to be taking a well-earned rest.

"They've got plenty of energy," Amelia said. "And Rose doesn't look grumpy anymore." In fact, lying on her side, blinking her dark eyes, Rose looked more relaxed and content than she had for a long time.

"I think she'll be a great mummy rabbit," said Izzy, smiling. Then her face fell. "But we're back at school tomorrow. I won't be able to spend much time with the baby rabbits at all!"

Amelia wished they had a few more days of holiday left to spend with the kits

The baby rabbits wriggled constantly, unlike their mum, who seemed to be taking a well-earned rest.

"They've got plenty of energy," Amelia said. "And Rose doesn't look grumpy anymore." In fact, lying on her side, blinking her dark eyes, Rose looked more relaxed and content than she had for a long time.

"I think she'll be a great mummy rabbit," said Izzy, smiling. Then her face fell. "But we're back at school tomorrow. I won't be able to spend much time with the baby rabbits at all!"

Amelia wished they had a few more days of holiday left to spend with the kits

too, but she tried to sound cheerful. "You can see them after school," she said.

Sam nodded. "Exactly, and tomorrow you'll be able to tell everyone all about them."

Izzy brightened. "You're right," she said. "Everyone will be so surprised when they hear about my real Easter Bunnies!"

CHAPTER FOUR

At school, Amelia and Sam listened
eagerly as Izzy told a huddle of their
classmates all about her kits. "They were
sleeping in a bundle when I left them,"
Izzy said proudly.

"What are you going to call them?"
Caleb asked.

"I don't know," Izzy said. "I've had loads of ideas, but I just can't decide!"

"Seats everyone," Miss Hafiz called, clapping her hands. Amelia's classmates quickly dispersed, and Amelia sat next to Sam. While Miss Hafiz held up her hand, waiting for quiet, Amelia opened her writing book and started to doodle a tiny rabbit with little stubby ears. As

she thought of the kits' funny, wrinkled little legs and squidgy-looking tummies, she found that she was fizzing with

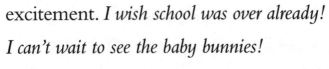

excitement. *I wish school was over already! I can't wait to see the baby bunnies!*

"Amelia Haywood?"

Hearing her name, Amelia blinked and looked up to find her teacher watching her, one eyebrow raised. The register was open, and Amelia got the impression it might not have been the first time her teacher had called her name.

Amelia winced. "Sorry, Miss Hafiz. I'm here."

Once their teacher had finished calling the register, chatter broke out again all over the classroom, but Miss Hafiz clapped her hands again, and the voices fell quiet.

"I hope you've all enjoyed your holidays," Miss Hafiz said. "But now it's time to concentrate on the new term ahead. We have something exciting planned! The whole school will be running a talent show. Anyone can enter,

and your talent can be anything – from dancing, to reciting poetry, to unicycling if you like! So, have a think, and if you're interested in performing, just sign your name on this sheet. I'll put it up on the wall by the door."

Miss Hafiz smiled. "And now, I would like you all to open your exercise books, and write about everything you've been up to over Easter break!"

After the morning's lessons, Sam, Amelia and Izzy sat together in the school lunch hall, munching sandwiches. Every table was packed, and the sounds of excited chatter and the clink of cutlery rang out all around them.

"Do you think you'll enter the talent competition?" Sam asked Izzy.

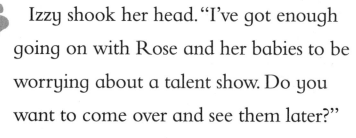

Izzy shook her head. "I've got enough going on with Rose and her babies to be worrying about a talent show. Do you want to come over and see them later?"

"Definitely!" Sam said.

"I was hoping you'd ask," Amelia said.

"How about you two?" Izzy asked. "Are you going to enter the talent show?"

Amelia shrugged. "I'd like to," she said, "but I'm not sure I really have a talent. I've never had dancing lessons or anything like that. I'll have to think about it."

"I know what I'm going to do!" Sam said. "I found my mum's juggling balls in the loft over the holidays. I've been practising and I'm starting to get the hang of it."

Just then, a round of applause broke out nearby. Amelia turned to see Dominic Donovan, a tall, dark-haired boy from the year above, standing at his table, with a cluster of his classmates gathered around him. As she watched, Dominic reached forwards and pulled a shiny coin from behind another boy's ear. *Ooohs* and *ahhhs* rose from the

group, followed by another round of applause.

"Wow – he's pretty good," Izzy said. "Let's go and watch." They quickly joined the students crowded around Dominic. Amelia leaned in, watching closely as he performed another magic trick with the coin, fluttering his fingers and making the coin vanish, only for it to reappear in his other hand.

"That's amazing!" Amelia said, her voice almost drowned out by claps and cheers. She couldn't see how he'd done it at all.

"Do you know any other tricks?" Izzy asked eagerly.

"Sure!" said Dominic, grinning. He flicked his hair back from his eyes, then made a fist with one hand and wiggled the fingers of the other hand over it. When he opened his fist, a deck of cards was nestled in his palm. Dominic shuffled the cards, then he fanned them out and held them towards Sam.

"Pick a card and look at it, but don't show me," Dominic said. "Then put it

back in the deck, wherever you want."

Sam eased a card out and peeked at it, then slid it back, near the middle of the deck.

Dominic folded the cards back together and shuffled them again. Then, resting one hand on top of the deck, he closed his eyes, frowning intently.

Suddenly, Dominic's eyes snapped open. "Sam, could you check your left-hand pocket?" he said.

Sam reached into his trouser pocket, and his eyes went round with surprise. He drew out a card, then held it up – it was the ace of clubs. "That's my card! How did you do that?" Sam asked,

blushing as the other
students gasped and
applauded.

Dominic tossed his
hair and tapped the side
of his nose. "A magician
never reveals his secrets."
Then he grinned. "It's
actually not that hard,"
he said. "It just takes a
lot of practise. I'm going to do a magic
act in the talent show, because I know
loads more tricks. How about you, Sam?
What are you going to do?"

As everyone looked at Sam, Amelia
saw her friend shrink back a little.

"Um … I was thinking of doing a juggling act," Sam mumbled.

"Nice! How about a demo?" Dominic said. "I bet we've got enough apples between us."

At least half a dozen hands waved pieces of fruit in Sam's direction. He  stepped back, and Amelia could almost feel the heat coming off his cheeks. "I … don't … My act isn't quite ready yet," Sam muttered.

"Ah, that's a shame," said Dominic. "But

there's loads of time to practise." He
fanned his cards out smoothly and slid
them back together again.

Amelia could see Sam was still
embarrassed.

"You OK?" Amelia whispered, as
everyone turned back to Dominic.

"Yeah," Sam said. "But I'm starting to
regret putting my name down for the
show! Now I've seen what Dominic can
do, my juggling seems a bit lame."

"Well, he certainly knows how to show
off," Amelia said, watching as Dominic
made the queen of hearts jump to the
top of the deck. Tiffany Banks giggled
and fluttered her eyelashes. "Anyhow, the

show is just supposed to be for fun."

"I guess," Sam said, managing half a smile.

"And you've still got ages to practise," Amelia said. "Why don't you bring your juggling balls over to mine later, and I'll help? Then we can visit Izzy and her bunnies!"

Sam grinned. "Deal!"

CHAPTER FIVE

"Mac! Bring that back!" Sam called, as his Westie bounded away with a juggling ball clenched firmly in his jaws.

Amelia leapt in front of the little dog, blocking his way. "Here, Mac!" she said, putting out her hand. Mac skidded to a stop and eyed her suspiciously, then set

off to race the other way around her gran's front garden.

"Give!" Sam tried. Mac bounded towards him and stopped neatly at his master's feet. But when Sam reached for the ball, the Westie turned his head stubbornly away. Amelia giggled. *He really doesn't want to let that ball go.*

Finally, Sam caught Mac by the collar and gently removed the ball from his dog's jaws.

"Right, I'm going to do it this time!" Sam said. Concentrating so hard that his tongue poked out from the corner of his mouth, Sam started to juggle.

Go, Sam! Amelia thought, as he caught

all three balls and threw them up again.
Sam caught the first one neatly. Amelia
winced as the second went wild, but Sam
just managed to snatch it from the air.
Go on! You can do it! But the third ball
flew way off course. Sam lunged for it
and batted it halfway across the garden.
Mac was after it in an instant.

Sam's shoulders sagged.

"Maybe it's the sun getting in your
eyes?" Amelia said. "And Mac keeps
distracting you. You might do better
inside."

"I can't," Sam said, grumpily. "Mum's
already banned me from practising at
home after I broke her crystal vase.

I don't want to get banned from your gran's house as well!"

Amelia tried to think of something encouraging to say. "Maybe it's like riding a bike," she said. "Once you get the hang of it, you'll probably never forget."

"*If* I get the hang of it," Sam said.

"You will!" Amelia said. "And at least you know what you're going to do in the show. I don't have a talent at all."

"Everyone has a talent," said Sam, firmly. "We just have to find yours."

"Hello, you two," a friendly voice called, and Amelia recognised it at once. *Miss Hafiz!* Amelia turned to see

her teacher smiling over the front gate.
A tall man wearing jeans and a t-shirt
stood beside her. He had the same kind
smile as Miss Hafiz, and he was holding
the hands of two small boys. They wore
identical football kits, and each had huge
dark-brown eyes, spiked dark hair and
identical mischievous grins.

"This is my brother, Uzair, and these
are his twins, Zafir and Ayaan," Miss
Hafiz said. Then she nodded at the balls
in Sam's hands. "I see you're practising
for the show. I can't wait to see your
juggling!"

"I'm not quite ready yet," Sam said,
shoving his juggling balls into his pockets.

68

"A dog!" One of the little boys cried as Mac scampered over to greet them, still carrying Sam's last ball.

"I'll lift him up so you can pet him if you like?" Sam offered.

"Did you hear that, boys?" Uzair said. "You can stroke the little dog, but you will have to be gentle."

Sam hefted Mac up and eased the slobbery ball from his jaws.

One of the twins reached out a hand and very gently tried to stroke Mac's head. Immediately, Mac lifted his nose and licked the child's fingers. The boy started to giggle hysterically. His brother

stroked the stiff fur on the back of Mac's neck.

"Oh! Can we get a dog too, Daddy?" he asked.

Miss Hafiz's brother laughed. "My boys are

crazy about animals," he told Sam and
Amelia. "We've promised them we'll get
a pet, but I think a dog might be too
much work."

"They do need quite a lot of training,"
Amelia said. "And walks!"

Mac started to scrabble in Sam's arms,
so he set him down. "Mac's great," Sam
said. "But he's definitely hard work.
He needs to go out twice a day, and
if I don't give him enough attention,
he finds his own fun – and that usually
isn't pretty!"

"Hmm, with twin boys already, a dog
might be a stretch too far," Uzair said.
"We need to start smaller. How about a

pet goldfish?" he asked his boys.

They both stared up at their father, open-mouthed with outrage, glowering from under their dark brows. Amelia saw Uzair's eyes twinkle. "Just kidding!" he said. "I'll have to keep thinking. But now we'd better get going. Say thank you to Auntie's students for letting you pet Mac."

After waving goodbye to Miss Hafiz, Uzair and the twins, Amelia glanced at her watch. It was already half past four! "Sam! We'd better get a move on, too!" she said. "We're supposed to be going to Izzy's house!"

Amelia was hot from running, and practically bursting with excitement as she and Sam reached Izzy's house. The door flew open before they had even knocked. But as Amelia caught sight of Izzy's face, pinched with worry, her excitement drained in an instant.

"What's wrong?" Amelia asked.

"I'm not sure," Izzy said, in a small voice. "But I don't think Rose is feeding her babies. Can you come and look?"

Amelia and Sam hurried after Izzy through to the garden. They found Izzy's mum crouched in front of the rabbit hutch, her face grave. Half dreading what she might see, Amelia knelt beside

Izzy's mum and peered through the wire mesh.

Rose was nibbling at the alfalfa hay in her bowl, her coat glossy and her eyes wide and clear. But her babies were a different story. All four lay curled together in the straw, as if trying to keep warm. Their bellies looked wrinkled and flat, and they were barely moving at all. Amelia swallowed hard. *Something's definitely wrong …*

"I know we're not supposed to disturb the babies," Izzy said. "But they weren't

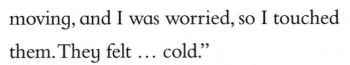

moving, and I was worried, so I touched them. They felt … cold."

Izzy's words sent a jolt of fear through Amelia. "We need to get them all to Animal Ark," she said. "Now!"

"But won't the surgery be shutting soon?" Izzy's mum asked.

"It doesn't matter," Amelia said. "The Hopes won't turn us away. This is a real emergency!"

CHAPTER SIX

Amelia's heart pounded as she pushed
open the door at Animal Ark. Izzy's mum
had driven them there, and now she
was carrying a shoebox with the baby
bunnies inside, while Izzy held Rose in
her carrier. Sam followed behind them,
his eyes wide with worry.

Inside the surgery they found Mr Hope reaching for the light switch. "Hello!" he said, leaving the lights on. "You caught us just in time – we were shutting up."

Mrs Hope was holding the surgery keys, but she put them in her pocket. "What's wrong?" she asked.

"It's Rose's babies," Izzy's mum said. She showed the vet the shoebox with the four kits inside, nestled in cotton wool. "We don't think they're feeding."

The Hopes both took a quick look at the babies, then exchanged a decisive nod. "We'll examine them now," Mr Hope said.

Mrs Hope unlocked her treatment

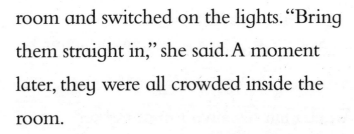

room and switched on the lights. "Bring them straight in," she said. A moment later, they were all crowded inside the room.

Izzy held tight to her mum's hand, and Sam and Amelia watched silently as Mrs Hope examined Rose while Mr Hope inspected the four little rabbits with a blue-gloved finger. The kits squirmed slightly, batting his finger with their tiny paws, then stopped moving.

"You were right to bring them in," Mr Hope said. "They haven't been feeding. If they had, they would be warm, and their bellies would be round and full."

"Unfortunately, Rose isn't producing

79

any milk," said Mrs Hope.

"But … that means they'll all die!" Izzy said, her eyes filling with tears. Amelia felt her own throat tighten.

"Don't worry," Mrs Hope said, kindly and firmly. "The babies should still be all right." She opened the treatment room fridge and took out a glass vial. "I'm going to give Rose an injection. It should stimulate her milk production. It's a good thing you noticed the problem when you did. The injection only works if it's given in the first 48 hours after birth."

Izzy looked at Amelia, her face suddenly very pale. "I'm so glad you knew to bring them straight here," she

said. "If we'd waited until the morning
…" She shuddered.

Amelia squeezed Izzy's arm. "They'll
be OK," she said, sounding surer than she
felt. *I just hope the injection works …*

Mr Hope scooped Rose from her
carrier and held her still on the table,
stroking the bunny with one hand to
keep her calm. Mrs Hope prepared her
injection, tapping the syringe to get rid

of bubbles. Then she gripped the fold of skin between Rose's shoulder blades, and quickly gave the jab. With Mr Hope still stroking her head, Rose didn't even seem to notice.

"Now, it's a waiting game," Mrs Hope said. "You can all go through to reception. We'll put Rose and her babies together in a pen. Before long, we should know if the injection has worked."

After using the reception phone to call their parents, Amelia and Sam settled down with Izzy and her mum to wait. In the quiet room, with its rows of empty

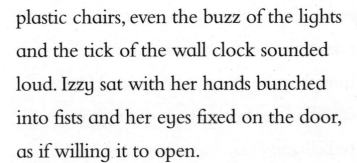

plastic chairs, even the buzz of the lights
and the tick of the wall clock sounded
loud. Izzy sat with her hands bunched
into fists and her eyes fixed on the door,
as if willing it to open.

We need to distract Izzy, Amelia thought.
Then she had an idea.

"Hey, Sam, how about some juggling
practice? You could use those cat toys."
She pointed at a display stand.

Sam looked puzzled at first, but Amelia
glanced pointedly at Izzy. Sam nodded,
catching on. "I guess I could give it a go."

He unhooked three colourful beanbag
mice, and began to juggle. Before long,
all three mice were scattered on the floor.

"Oops," said Sam, sheepishly.

Izzy gave a small smile, and her hunched shoulders relaxed just a little.

"It's tricky without proper juggling balls," said Sam. He scooped up the mice and tried again. Amelia, Izzy and her mum watched and clapped whenever he managed to keep the cat toys up in the air for a few throws.

Finally, at just after seven o'clock, the door to the backroom opened. Everyone fell suddenly silent – so quiet Amelia could almost hear the thud

of her own heart. But then Mr Hope put his head through the door and smiled. All the tension suddenly dissolved, and Amelia felt dizzy with relief. *They're going to be OK!*

"Come and take a look," Mr Hope said softly. Izzy went first with her mum. Amelia and Sam followed close behind. They all huddled together and peered into a straw-filled pen.

Inside, Amelia could see Rose lying quietly and munching on a mouthful of hay, while her four babies snuggled up close to her in a squirming bundle. Their noses were buried deep in Rose's fur, and they looked rounder and pinker already.

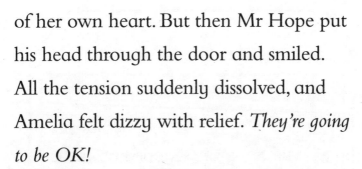

Their tiny paws twitched and batted as they fed.

"It worked!" Izzy said, throwing her arms around her mum.

"Thank goodness," Izzy's mum said, holding her daughter tight. Amelia and Sam exchanged a misty-eyed smile. Even Mr and Mrs Hope looked a little choked up. "But what went wrong?" Izzy's mum asked. "Why didn't Rose have any milk?"

"It's hard to be sure," Mrs Hope said. "Something might have happened soon after the birth that made Rose feel stressed. Or it might just be bad luck. Rabbits can be quite unpredictable with their first litter. Once they've had the

babies, they don't always know what to do with them."

"Oh! I wish we could keep them all," Izzy said, her eyes fixed on the feeding kits.

"We'll have to see," Izzy's mum said. "Don't forget, they'll grow up to be as big as Rose. I'm not sure that we'll have enough space."

Thinking of Izzy's small back garden, already half-filled with the run and two rabbit hutches, Amelia wasn't sure either. But she was sure about one thing. "I'll do anything I can to help," she said.

"That's it!" Sam said. He turned to Amelia with a knowing grin.

"That's what?" she asked, confused.

"Your special talent," Sam said. "It's helping people – you always know the right thing to say and do. You should help out at the talent show! I bet there's a lot of work to be done backstage."

"He's right!" Izzy said. "You could help run the show! You'd be brilliant at it, Amelia. You'd make sure everything went to plan and stop anyone getting too nervous!"

Hmm, Amelia thought. *That*

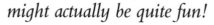

might actually be quite fun!

"*Awww*, thanks guys," she said, smiling. "I'd love to help out. That's an absolutely brilliant idea!"

Amelia peeked again at the four little rabbits, nosing at their mother's fur and jostling against each other for space. They already looked stronger. She felt a warm, satisfied glow inside. *Helping out is the best feeling in the world ... especially when animals are involved!*

STORY TWO:
The Talent Show

CHAPTER ONE

Amelia pulled her coat tightly around her as she headed out for morning break with Izzy and Sam. The blustery wind whipped at her hair and made the scattered clouds race across the sky. It was a bright and gusty Friday, six weeks after Izzy's baby rabbits had been born.

Only a week until the talent show! Amelia thought. *I hope everything will be ready in time!* She'd spent the last few days labelling and organizing costumes and props and making sure all the music for the acts was ready. But there was still a lot to do.

"You *have* to show me the line-up," Sam begged Amelia. "I need to know when I'm on." Amelia had just finished writing out the final running order with Miss Hafiz. She took a folded copy from her coat pocket and smoothed it out for Sam, holding it tight against the wind. He ran his eyes down the list and groaned loudly.

"I'm right after Dominic!" Sam said. "Seriously, I can't go after him! He's too good."

"You've been practising loads," Izzy said. "It'll be fine!"

Remembering Sam's last juggling session at the park, Amelia felt a twinge of doubt.

"Don't worry," she said. "I'll swap you round. Dominic's act can be last. I'm sure he'll be happy to do the grand finale."

"Thank you!" Sam said. "I suppose I'd better get a bit more practise in now."

After finding a quiet corner of the playground, Amelia and Izzy stood well back while Sam took his juggling balls from his pockets. He looked less nervous than when he'd started, and he even managed to keep his tongue out of sight.

Amelia held her breath as the three balls went up, one after another. Sam managed to catch them all, and then again, getting into a rhythm. His eyes were shining, and Amelia was just about to start cheering, but suddenly someone called "Hey!"

loudly across the playground. Sam fumbled a catch and all three balls came tumbling down.

They all turned to see Dominic Donovan striding towards them, his hands in his pockets. Amelia was surprised to see the older boy on his own for once. Since he'd started showing off his magic tricks, Dominic always seemed to be surrounded by a crowd.

"Sorry if I distracted you, Sam," Dominic said. Amelia looked hard at Dominic, but he seemed sincere.

"That's OK," Sam said, shrugging.

Dominic took a coin from his pocket and started playing with it, making it

appear and disappear between his fingers as he turned to Izzy. "I heard you've got some baby rabbits. I was wondering if they're up for adoption?"

Izzy grinned. "I've got four – two boys and two girls. They are so cute. And they've all got different personalities. I really wish I could keep them all!" Izzy's smile faded. "Unfortunately, they're getting too big. My mum says we don't have enough room. Would you like to meet them?"

"What colour are they?" asked Dominic. "Do you have any white ones?"

Izzy frowned. "No. Both of the girls are

grey. One of the
boys is piebald –
white with black
patches – and the
other one is light
brown."

Dominic looked
disappointed for a
moment, then nodded thoughtfully.
"I guess light brown could work," he
said. Then he smiled. "Yes! I could call
it Presto!"

Amelia felt a twinge of unease. *Why's
he so bothered about the rabbit's colour?*

"You can come and take a look at
him after school if you like," Izzy said.

"But you'll have to get a hutch."

"Of course," Dominic said. "I'll pop by today, if that's OK?"

"All right," Izzy said. "I live at 24 Sycamore Road. I'll see you later."

Dominic grinned and nodded. "Awesome!" he said. Then he turned and slouched away, his hands still in his pockets.

"What was that about?" Amelia said frowning. "How can he know which rabbit he wants when he hasn't even met them yet?" She remembered the feeling she'd had when she had adopted her pet kitten, Star. *Surely you pick a pet by falling in love with it, not what colour it is!*

"I guess it is a bit weird," Izzy said. "But Dominic seems nice, even if he's a show-off. I think we should give him a chance. After all, I do need to re-home the rabbits. I've been putting it off as long as I can, but they're getting cramped in the hutch. I don't want them fighting or trying to escape like Tulip did."

"You're right," Amelia said, remembering how upset Izzy had been when Tulip went missing, before she had adopted Poppy and Rose. "But don't worry! Sam and I will help. We're expert animal re-homers. And your baby rabbits are all so cute… we're sure to find perfect homes for them all in no time!"

CHAPTER TWO

"So, about your show," Amelia's dad said over the phone, on Saturday morning. "I'd love to come and see it!"

Amelia felt a tingle of excitement at the thought of her dad coming to the talent show. "I'm not actually going to be on stage," she reminded him.

"But I'll know it's you making the show run smoothly," her dad said. "It's important to you — so it's important to me. And I can take you back to York after the show."

"Thanks, Dad," Amelia said, grinning. "It'll be awesome to have you there." Just then, the doorbell rang. "That will be Sam," Amelia told her dad. "I'd better go. We've got to find homes for some baby rabbits."

Amelia's dad chuckled. "Sounds like a typical Saturday in Welford then," he said. "I'll see you on Friday!"

Amelia answered the door to find Sam smiling back at her, holding up a memory stick. "I've finished making the poster," he said. "Are you ready to print it out?"

Amelia nodded. "I've got Mum's laptop and printer set up in the dining room."

It didn't take long for Sam to load up the poster he'd made.

"*Awww!*" Amelia said, when she saw the pictures Izzy had sent through. The two grey rabbits sat together, looking timidly at the camera with their big dark eyes. The brown rabbit, the smallest of the litter, had been caught mid-nibble. He looked a bit goofy, with a huge dandelion leaf hanging from his mouth. The piebald rabbit, the boldest of the four kits, had come right up to the camera, as if he was trying to sniff the lens. Amelia smiled to herself. With his dark, curious eyes and patchy fur, the

black-and-white bunny was secretly her favourite.

Amelia clicked the mouse button to start printing. "It's perfect. We can put a few up at school and one at Animal Ark."

"They're so cute we should get loads of interest," Sam said, as the printer whirred into life.

"I hope so," Amelia said. "Bunnies are perfect pets, especially for busy families."

"And far less work than a dog!" Sam added.

Suddenly, Amelia felt as if a light had pinged on in her brain. "You're a genius, Sam!" she exclaimed.

Sam frowned, puzzled. "I may be a

genius, but you've totally lost me,"
he said.

"Wait until this afternoon when we're
at Izzy's. I'll explain then," Amelia told
him. *I really hope this plan works!* she
thought to herself.

Amelia sat on the lawn, bathed in
afternoon sunshine, watching Izzy's
rabbits play on the grass. Cardboard
tubes and wicker toys were scattered
among bits of carrot and fruit. She and
Sam had visited often over the last few
weeks, to help the kits get used to people.
And Amelia suddenly realised with a

pang that if everything went to plan, this might be one of the last times they were all together.

Sam was holding a grape out for one of the little grey bunnies. Its whiskers quivered as it nibbled at the fruit. Izzy had managed to coax the light brown bunny onto her lap where it was gnawing on a bit of carrot.

The piebald rabbit was peeking out from a cardboard tube. Amelia extended

 her fingers, then held her breath as he hopped out of the tube and across the

grass, his eyes bright with interest. As soon as the rabbit was close enough, Amelia slowly reached out to stroke him. The rabbit's coat felt warm from the sun, and unbelievably soft.

"Each time I get the babies out, they seem tamer," Izzy said, stroking the brown rabbit as he ate. "Which is just as well, because Dominic's coming to fetch this little guy in a bit."

A few moments later, the doorbell rang. Amelia, Izzy and Sam exchanged hopeful grins.

"You look after the rabbits, while we get the door," Amelia told Sam. "Let's all keep our fingers crossed!"

"Hello," Miss Hafiz said, as Izzy opened the door. Her brother, Uzair, stood next to her smiling, with Ayaan and Zafir.

"We've come for our surprise!" one of the boys said.

Miss Hafiz nodded. "We're very interested to know why you have invited us … and what the surprise might be."

"Come through!" Izzy said. She turned to Uzair. "We remembered what you said about Ayaan and Zafir being animal crazy, and we thought they might like to come and meet my rabbits."

"Bunnies!" one of the boys gasped.

"Can we stroke them?" his twin chimed in.

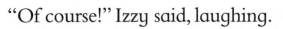

"Of course!" Izzy said, laughing.

When they reached the door to the garden, Uzair stopped, and looked sternly at each of his twin boys in turn. "Remember," he said, "soft voices and gentle hands!"

As soon as they stepped into the garden, the boys froze as still as statues. They stared at the rabbits in awed silence, their cheeky grins gone and their eyes wide.

"They look so soft!" one of the boys whispered at last.

"Come and sit down," Izzy told them. "You can hold the rabbits in your lap."

While Izzy led the boys over to where

Sam was stroking the two grey baby rabbits, Amelia stayed back with Uzair and Miss Hafiz. "There was another reason we invited you," Amelia told them, her pulse suddenly quickening. She spoke quietly, so the twins wouldn't hear. "We remembered that you were trying to find a pet for the boys," she said. "One that was less work than a dog but more fun than a goldfish … Well, Izzy's baby rabbits need adopting. The brown one is already spoken for, but the other three still need to find homes. What do you think?"

Uzair frowned thoughtfully, then glanced over to where the two boys sat,

each very gently stroking a grey bunny that was nestled in their lap. Amelia balled her fists. *Please say yes!* she pleaded silently.

At last, Uzair let out a theatrical sigh. "They do look smitten!" he said, grinning. "And I know my wife loves rabbits – she used to have some when she was small."

"Those two rabbits are so similar to

each other, they could be twins too," Miss Hafiz said. "I think it's a great idea."

Uzair raised his voice, speaking to his boys. "How would you two like to adopt a pet rabbit each?"

Ayaan and Zafir looked up at their dad, their eyes shining with excitement. "Yes, please!" they both said.

Her chest swelling with happiness, Amelia glanced over to Sam and Izzy and gave them a big thumbs up. Sam and Izzy high-fived, their grins as wide as Amelia's.

Amelia smiled as she watched the twins play with the bunnies. The boys' faces glowed with happiness, but they kept their movements slow and calm as they offered the rabbits treats and stroked their soft grey fur.

Three down, one to go, Amelia thought. Kneeling, she beckoned the piebald bunny towards her with a piece of carrot, then stroked his velvety back. "I haven't forgotten you," Amelia whispered. "I promise I'll find you a wonderful home too!"

CHAPTER THREE

A few days later, Amelia and Sam
exchanged nervous glances as they
waited outside Dominic's house which
had a blue van and a huge, shiny
motorbike filling up the drive. *I hope he
doesn't mind us popping by …*

Dominic opened the door, holding

Presto carefully in one arm. The bunny blinked at Amelia and Sam with its big, dark eyes. "Hi," Dominic said, frowning at them slightly.

"We've come to bring you a bag of rabbit treats from Animal Ark, to help you get Presto settled," Sam said.

Dominic's face brightened. "That's really kind of you," he said. "Do you guys want to come in?"

"That would be great," Amelia said. "We can take the treats to Presto's hutch if you like. Where are you keeping him?"

Dominic led them into a hallway, easing between a pair of bikes on one side, and a bulging coat rack on the other. "His hutch is up in my room," Dominic said. "There isn't a lot of space anywhere else." Just then an older boy, dark-haired like Dominic but much broader, thundered down the stairs. He had a football kit bag slung over his shoulder, and as he passed, he ruffled Dominic's hair.

Dominic slapped the boy's hand away.

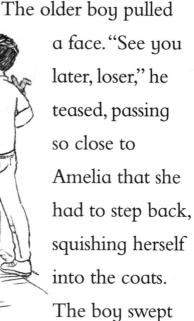

"Get off!" he said.

The older boy pulled a face. "See you later, loser," he teased, passing so close to Amelia that she had to step back, squishing herself into the coats. The boy swept out of the house, banging the door shut behind him.

"Don't mind my brother," Dominic said. "He thinks he's a football legend just because he's captain of the school

team. Come through to the living room. I'll bring Presto down. You can hold him if you like." Sam and Amelia followed Dominic into a sitting room, where all the surfaces were cluttered with trophies and photo frames. A tall girl with long dark hair was draped over the leather couch. She had a mobile phone clamped to her ear and was painting her toenails with her free hand.

"Get out!" the girl mouthed, gesturing sharply towards the door.

Dominic rolled his eyes. "My room it is, then," he said.

As Dominic led the way up the stairs, Amelia noticed the framed photographs

 hanging on
the wall. She
spotted several of
Dominic's older
brother, holding
football trophies.

There were lots of his sister too, wearing
gymnastics costumes, or on horseback,
decorated with ribbons. Only a couple
of the photos looked like they might be
of Dominic.

Amelia felt suddenly sad for him. She
always thought having a sibling might
be fun. *But it can't be easy being the youngest
…* Maybe that's why he was always
trying to impress people with his tricks.

Dominic's room was tidy, but small, and Presto's cage took up a lot of the floor space. A cabin bed stood at the other side of the room, with shelves and a desk underneath, all covered in neatly arranged magical props – cups and cards, rings and balls. Even Dominic's duvet was decorated with playing cards. On the wall, Amelia could see a poster of a famous magician pulling a rabbit out of a hat.

Hmm... Something had been nagging at Amelia ever since Dominic had asked about adopting a rabbit. Now she couldn't resist asking him about it. "So why did you want a white rabbit,

particularly?" she asked.

Dominic grinned. "Take a seat and I'll show you!" He gestured to a large beanbag in the corner. Amelia sat down next to Sam, feeling uneasy. Sam shot her a puzzled glance, and she could tell he was worried too.

With Presto still tucked under his arm, Dominic crossed to his cabin bed and pulled a top hat and a magic wand from a cubby hole. He set them down on his desk, then placed Presto inside. Amelia frowned.

"This is going to be the finale for my magic act!" Dominic said. He waved his magic wand. "Abracadabra!" he said.

Then he reached into the top hat to scoop Presto out.

"No!" Amelia cried, jumping to her feet. "You can't use Presto in the talent show!"

Sam was on his feet too. "Presto isn't

a stage prop!" Sam said. "He's an animal!"

Dominic snatched his hand back, looking startled. Then his face clouded over. "You're just jealous!" he said.

"Because you know my act's going to be the best in the show."

"That's got nothing to do with it," Amelia said. "Izzy never would have let you adopt Presto if she'd known you only wanted to use him in a magic act."

"That's not the only reason!" Dominic said, blushing now. "I wanted a pet, too. But I don't see why I can't include him in my show, if I'm not hurting him."

"Rabbits are timid animals," Amelia said. Her heart was pounding, and the words poured out of her in an angry rush. "A show with lots of people and bright lights will terrify Presto. It's a terrible idea."

Sam put out a hand. "Listen," he said, in a softer tone, "you could still do the same trick, but with a toy rabbit."

"The *only* way you can do that trick is with a toy rabbit!" Amelia snapped, her face burning. She could see Dominic was upset, but she was so furious it was hard to feel sorry for him. *How could he even think of using Presto in the show?*

Dominic's face crumpled, but then he shrugged. "Fine," he said.

"So, you'll use a toy?" Amelia said.

"Yeah. I'll use a toy," Dominic muttered.

"The trick will still look really cool," Sam said.

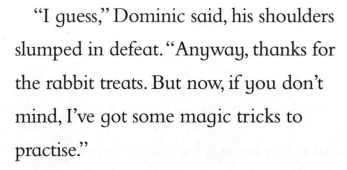

"I guess," Dominic said, his shoulders slumped in defeat. "Anyway, thanks for the rabbit treats. But now, if you don't mind, I've got some magic tricks to practise."

After Dominic had led them out and closed the door behind them, Sam and Amelia exchanged a look. "I'm so glad we came!" Sam said. "Imagine what would have happened if Dominic had brought poor Presto to school."

"Hmm," Amelia said, still feeling uneasy. Had Dominic really understood what was wrong with putting Presto in his show? She really hoped so …

133

CHAPTER FOUR

Even from where Amelia stood outside the school lunch hall, the clamour of voices was almost deafening. The scent of baked beans wafted out, mingled with the soggy cucumber smell of lunchboxes. She reached up to stick her poster to the wall with tape. As she smoothed it out,

she looked again at the close-up shot of the little piebald bunny with his velvety ears and big, dark eyes.

Amelia let out a sigh. *No home yet.* She'd felt sure that she and Sam would find the rabbit somewhere to live this week. But it was already Thursday, and no one had shown any interest. She had even emailed the poster to her dad, in case he knew anyone at work who might want a rabbit. But she was beginning to lose hope.

Just as Amelia was about to turn away from the poster, Tiffany Banks swept out of the lunch hall, surrounded by a group of her friends.

"*Aww!* Bunny rabbits," Tiffany said. "Are there any left?"

Amelia felt a spark of hope. "This one is," she said, pointing to the cute piebald kit.

Tiffany wrinkled her nose. "How about the little grey ones?" she asked. "They're so pretty!"

"No, they've already been adopted."

"Or the brown one?" Tiffany asked.

"Dominic Donovan's got that one," Amelia said.

Tiffany sighed. "Never mind, then.

A blotchy one won't look good in photos. Besides, Sparkle Barkle would be jealous." Sparkle was Tiffany's dog – a cute little Bichon Frise with fluffy white curls. Tiffany turned to her friends with a swish of her silky ponytail. "Let's go practise our act!" she said. "We need it to be perfect for tomorrow!"

As Amelia watched Tiffany go, she found herself clenching her teeth. *What is wrong with people? Why does the colour of a rabbit's fur matter so much?*

Just then, the bell rang, signalling the end of lunch. Amelia took a deep breath and forced herself to calm down. *I've promised I'll find the last bunny a home, and I won't give up. But right now, I need to concentrate on the show.*

In the dimly lit wings of the stage, with music playing beyond the closed curtains and her checklist in hand, Amelia had managed to put her worries about the piebald rabbit out of her mind.

It was the final rehearsal before the talent show and the excitement of the performers was contagious. A line of students waiting to be called on stage stood nearby. Sam was at the back, passing his juggling balls nervously from hand to hand.

Amelia frowned. *Where's Dominic?* she thought, biting her lip. He was supposed to be behind Sam, but he was nowhere to be seen.

As the music finished, a smattering of applause broke out. From her station near the curtain, Miss Hafiz beckoned the dancers offstage. Amelia turned to direct the girls through a side door to where they could change their costumes, when she suddenly heard a clamour of excited voices.

Glancing back, she saw the students who had been waiting in the wings all crowding around Dominic. He was carrying a box draped in black velvet.

Dominic set the box down on a table of props. "Prepare to meet Presto, the magic bunny!" he cried. Then he drew back the velvet and scooped Presto out of the box.

Amelia felt her stomach drop. She and Sam exchanged horrified glances as the huddle of students cooed over the rabbit.

"What is going on here?" Miss Hafiz said, turning sharply. The cluster of students all fell silent as Miss Hafiz's kind face clouded over. "Put that rabbit away immediately!" their teacher said sternly. "You know you're not allowed to bring pets into school."

"But I need Presto for my act!" Dominic protested, holding his rabbit close to his chest.

Amelia heard a low, rumbling, growl. With a jolt of alarm, she realised it was coming from Presto. But before she could do anything, Dominic let out a shriek. "He bit me!" He snatched his hand away and lost his grip on the bunny.

Amelia watched in shock as the rabbit
fell, hit the floor and let out shrill squeal.

Oh, no! Presto!

CHAPTER FIVE

As the crowd of students drew back in alarm, Amelia darted towards Presto. The little brown rabbit was sitting very still, trembling, with his eyes half closed.

"I think he's hurt!" Amelia said, kneeling down to take a closer look.

"We'd better take him to the vet right

away," Miss Hafiz said. She was inspecting Dominic's hand. "And this needs a wash and a plaster."

Dominic stared at the blood oozing from his finger, his face flushed bright red. *If he'd left Presto at home, none of this would have happened!* thought Amelia. Then she noticed that Dominic's eyes were shining with tears. She took a deep breath. *He didn't hurt Presto on purpose,* Amelia told herself. *And that bite*

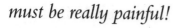

must be really painful!

A few minutes later, Miss Hafiz had left the class with another teacher and was driving Sam, Amelia and Dominic to Animal Ark. Sandwiched between Sam and Amelia in the backseat, Dominic's face looked grey with worry. His eyes were fixed on Presto, who was shivering in a nest of coloured scarves on his lap.

"Why didn't you use a soft toy like you said you would?" Amelia asked him.

Dominic glanced up at her. "I was going to," he said. "But I tried it and my brother said it looked rubbish without a real rabbit. I thought Presto would be fine as long as I was gentle with him …"

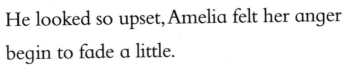

He looked so upset, Amelia felt her anger begin to fade a little.

"Is your finger all right?" Sam asked Dominic.

"It just needed a plaster," Dominic said. "I'm more worried about Presto. He's injured and it's all my fault." Dominic's voice cracked as he spoke, and Amelia saw him blink back tears. *He really does care about Presto!* she realised.

"The Hopes are amazing," Amelia told him, as Miss Hafiz pulled up outside the surgery. "If anyone can help Presto, they can."

They all filed into the waiting room at Animal Ark. Julia looked up from the

desk and frowned with concern.

"A visit in school time?" she said, to Miss Hafiz. "This must be an emergency."

"I'm afraid so," Miss Hafiz said. "Dominic's rabbit is injured." Amelia glanced around the reception area and noticed with relief that there weren't many patients waiting to be seen.

Julia nodded. "Mr Hope is free. I'll let him know you're here." The receptionist picked up the phone on her desk, and a moment later, Mr Hope opened his examination room door and beckoned them all inside.

"What happened?" Mr Hope asked, once Dominic had set Presto down on

the treatment
table. The
rabbit's eyes
were almost
shut now, and
he sat stiffly
in his nest of
scarves, still quivering all over.

"Presto has taken a tumble," Miss Hafiz
said.

"He's been like this ever since," Amelia
added. "Just sitting still and shivering."

Mr Hope nodded. "He's in shock," he
said. "I'll need to do a full examination
to find out what's wrong. Did he fall
very far?"

"From my hands," Dominic mumbled. "I was standing, and the floor was quite hard."

Mr Hope pulled on a pair of gloves, then very gently felt Presto's tummy, and all along the length of his spine. Presto's breathing was shallow, and his whiskers trembled. Amelia squeezed her hands together. *Please be all right …*

When Mr Hope touched the bunny's front left leg, Presto tensed, squeezing his eyes firmly shut. Mr Hope looked up with a sigh.

"I'm afraid that Presto might have a broken leg," he said. "We're going to need an X-Ray to be sure, but I think that he may need an operation."

Oh, no! thought Amelia.

"Will he be all right?" Dominic asked. His voice was shaking, and when Amelia glanced at him, she saw that his hands were trembling, too.

Mr Hope nodded. "There are no internal injuries, and the fracture feels like a simple one. I expect Presto to make a full recovery." Then he frowned. "But tell me, how exactly did this happen?"

Miss Hafiz raised an eyebrow and looked pointedly at Dominic. He flushed, and stared at his feet.

"I brought Presto into school as part of a magic act," Dominic admitted at last.

The kindly vet's frown deepened.

Dominic looked up and met Mr Hope's stern gaze. "I know I shouldn't have done it," he said. "I didn't think  it would go so wrong. I'll never do anything like that again."

"I'm glad to hear it," Mr Hope said. "Animals aren't props to be used for our entertainment. Having a pet is a big responsibility. Presto's wellbeing and happiness depends on you. And right now, I'm afraid he's a very scared, unhappy little bunny."

Dominic swallowed hard. "I'm so sorry," he said. He glanced towards Sam and Amelia. "They tried to warn me, but I thought it would be OK. Now I feel terrible! I never meant for Presto to get hurt."

"Well, it's a good thing to learn from your mistakes," Mr Hope said more gently. "I'll give Presto an injection now, to control the pain."

Dominic's eyes filled with tears and he looked back at his feet. "Please make him better," he whispered.

Amelia felt the last of her anger

drain away. *Poor Dominic!* "You know, you don't need a rabbit to impress people," she said. "Your magic tricks are amazing."

Dominic sighed. "I just wanted to show my family what I can do. But I didn't think about what was best for Presto."

"Everyone's going to love your act," Sam said. "You are seriously talented. Maybe you could pull something else out of your hat? Something weird. Like a toaster. Or maybe a bowling ball?"

Dominic managed a teary smile.

"Or how about a cricket bat?" Miss Hafiz said.

"Hey, what about a slice of pizza?" Mr Hope suggested, grinning.

Amelia and Sam giggled, and soon Dominic was smiling too. "Actually, that would be kind of funny," he said.

"Now, I'm going to take Presto for his treatment," Mr Hope told them. "I expect you all need to be heading back to school – after all, you've a talent show to prepare for. Dominic, Presto will be ready for you and your parents to collect tomorrow, any time after school."

"Have you had any luck finding a

home for the last rabbit?" Miss Hafiz
asked later, as they drove back.

Amelia shook her head. "I'm hoping
that with so many people coming to the
show tomorrow, someone will see one of
our posters and want to adopt him."

At the thought of the piebald bunny,
with his twitching nose and inquisitive
eyes, Amelia's heart gave a squeeze.
*Surely someone will want him … He's so
adorable!*

CHAPTER SIX

The following night, Amelia stood backstage just behind the curtain. She felt hot from rushing about, collecting props and directing people on and off stage, and her tummy was fluttering with nerves. Most of the evening's acts had already performed, but the show was far from over. Peeking around the curtain, Amelia could see her mum and gran smiling as they watched Tiffany and her friends dance. Amelia's dad was there too, grinning broadly and nodding in time to the music.

With the stage lights on and music blaring, the school hall seemed almost like a real theatre. Standing at Amelia's side, Sam jiggled nervously up and down. Dominic was checking through his props at a trestle table. He looked pale and serious, his dark brows drawn together in concentration.

"Can you see my parents?" Sam whispered to Amelia.

"To the left," she told him.

Sam peered through the curtain. When he turned back to her his eyes looked huge in the dim light. "There are so many people out there!"

"They all want it to go well." Amelia said. "Focus on your act. You'll be fine."

Sam managed a nervous smile.

The soundtrack to Tiffany's dance routine finished, and she and her friends all took a bow, blowing kisses to the crowd as applause rang out.

"You're on," Amelia told Sam, as the dancers left the stage.

Sam took a deep, shivery breath. "Here goes nothing," he said. Then he stepped through the curtain and into the light. Amelia peeked around the side of the curtain to watch, her whole body thrumming with nerves.

An expectant silence filled the hall. Sam stood still for a moment, weighing his leather balls in his hands. Then he started to juggle. Amelia almost couldn't bring herself to watch. But even though

one ball went wide, Sam managed to catch it and keep going. Amelia could see her friend's stiff posture loosening up and his shoulders relaxing. His throws and catches fell into an easy rhythm that Amelia had never seen him do before. Then, suddenly, he threw one ball up high ... And caught it!

Cheers went up from the crowd, but Sam carried on, adding a few more trick throws, before catching all five balls and ending with a bow.

A huge round of applause filled the hall as Sam shuffled bashfully offstage.

"That was brilliant!" Amelia said.

Sam looked at his feet, smiling shyly.

"Did you really think so?" he asked.

"Definitely!" Amelia said. "You nailed it!" she lifted her hand. Sam grinned and gave her a high five.

Amelia turned to Dominic. "You're on next," she told him. "The grand finale!"

Waiting by the curtain, Dominic nodded. He closed his eyes and took a deep breath. Then, smiling broadly, he strode on to the stage. "Ladies and gentlemen!" he said, in a loud, clear voice. "Prepare ... to be astonished!"

Watching from behind the scenes, Amelia and Sam couldn't see all of Dominic's tricks, but the crowd's gasps of amazement told them he was doing well.

Amelia saw him pull a string of coloured handkerchiefs from his sleeve, then make a bouquet of flowers appear out of thin air.

She spotted Dominic's family sitting near the front of the hall. His mum's face was glowing with pride, and even his older brother and sister looked impressed, nodding with approval at the end of each trick.

As the magic act reached its close, Dominic lifted the top hat from his head. Sam and Amelia exchanged an anxious look. *What was he going to pull out?* Amelia wondered. After a pause that seemed to go on forever, Dominic

reached into the hat,
and pulled out…
a takeaway pizza
box! He opened
the box, showing a
whole pizza inside,
complete with
toppings. Amelia and
Sam gasped as the

crowd went wild, clapping and cheering.
How on earth did he do that? Amelia
thought, amazed.

But there was no time to think it over.
Miss Hafiz was leading all the acts back
into the wings, ready to go on stage
for a final bow. The teacher beckoned

to Amelia, and she joined them on stage, slipping into place beside Sam. Exhilaration and pride fizzed through her as she stood with her friends onstage and gazed out at all the happy smiling faces in the audience. Cheers and applause rang through the hall. *We did it!* she realized, grinning. *The talent show was a big success!*

Afterwards, Amelia made her way into
the hall, where squash and biscuits were
being served. She squeezed past huddles
of people, until she spotted Mum and
Gran, drinking squash with her dad.

"That was brilliant!" Mum said.

Gran nodded. "I never knew the young
people of Welford had so much talent."

"And it ran like clockwork!" Amelia's
dad added. "Thanks to our very talented
stage manager!"

"Thanks, Dad!" Amelia said, wrapping
him in a hug. Just then Amelia spotted
Miss Hafiz heading towards them. Uzair
and his twins hurried behind her, along

with a lady wearing a blue headscarf. Amelia guessed she must be Sara, the twins' mum.

"You did a great job today, Amelia," Miss Hafiz said. "We couldn't have done it without your help!"

"I liked Sam's juggling!" Uzair said.

"Mummy! Tell her about the rabbits!" one of the twins said, swinging on his mother's arm.

Sara smiled. "I understand I have you and your friends to thank for our wonderful new pets," she said. She got out her phone, tapped the screen, then passed it down to one of the twins. The two boys crowded close to Amelia, showing her the pictures on the phone.

"My rabbit's called Jo Jo," one of the boys said.

"And mine is called Nina," the other blurted. "Look, we got them a big house with lots of toys, but they like playing with kitchen roll tubes the best. They roll them around!"

Amelia couldn't help smiling as she glanced from the boys' excited faces to

the pictures of the little grey rabbits on the phone. "I'm so happy the rabbits found such good friends to look after them!" she told the boys.

As Uzair, Sara and Miss Hafiz ushered the twins away, Dominic quickly took their place. "I'm glad I found you," Dominic said. "I didn't get a chance to tell you before the show, but we collected Presto after school, and he's doing really well. He's got a plaster on his leg, but Mr Hope says it will come off soon."

"That's brilliant news!" Amelia said. "And your act was amazing. I have no idea where you hid that pizza!"

Dominic winked. "It was magic, of

course!" he said. "Hey, if you and Sam would like to come and see Presto again, that would be awesome. I picked up some toys for him from Animal Ark. I'm going to put him first from now on."

Amelia watched Dominic as he headed off to see his family. *He really does have a good heart,* she thought. *I think Presto will be happy with him after all.*

"It sounds like your bunny re-homing project is going brilliantly!" Amelia's dad said, as they joined the queue of people leaving the hall. Amelia sighed, her spirits dipping.

"Almost," she said. "But there's still one bunny left."

"I wouldn't be so sure."

Amelia looked sharply into her dad's smiling face and felt a flicker of hope. "What do you mean?" she asked. But her dad just grinned harder and carried on shuffling forwards.

As they stepped outside into the cool evening air, the press of people dispersed and Amelia saw Izzy and her mum walking towards them. Izzy was holding an animal carrier. Inside, Amelia could just make out the black and white patches of the piebald rabbit. She looked again at her dad and saw that his eyes were twinkling.

"All your excitement about animals

has got me
thinking how nice
it would be to have
a pet of my own,"
said Dad. "So I
had a chat with
Izzy and her mum.
They've agreed
I can adopt the
last rabbit! From
everything you've told me about him, I
feel like I know him already. I'm going
to call him Charlie."

"No way!" Amelia cried. *I'll get to see
Charlie every time I visit Dad!* she suddenly
realised. Her chest felt like it might burst

with happiness. *A cat in Welford, and a rabbit in York … I can't believe how lucky I am to have two pets!*

The show had run like clockwork. Sam's juggling was a triumph. And best of all, the rabbits had all gone to happy homes.

This has been the most magical day ever! Amelia thought, as they headed off to take Charlie to his new home.

The End

Read Amelia and Sam's first
bunny adventure!

ANIMAL ARK

Bunny Trouble

Lucy Daniels

Amelia Haywood leaned into the car and gave her dad a hug.

"Be good for Mum and Gran," said Dad. "And if you can't be good …"

"… be careful!" Amelia finished, and Dad chuckled. Amelia was still getting used to not living with Dad any more. After the divorce, he had stayed in their old house in York, while Amelia and Mum had moved in with Gran in the countryside. He always said the same thing when he said goodbye to her.

Dad ruffled Amelia's long, blonde hair. "See you Saturday after next," he said. "Good luck at school. You'll be fine."

Amelia's stomach squirmed. Her first

day at her new school was tomorrow.

After Dad had driven away, Amelia turned towards the red front door of her new home. There was a hawthorn tree by the porch, with a blackbird pecking at the feeder that hung there. Bees were crawling hungrily over a clump of lavender. After a weekend in York, with its crowded city streets and bustling shops, it felt strange to be back in the countryside and among all the animals again.

Amelia opened and shut the front door quietly, so she wouldn't disturb the blackbird, and went back into the kitchen. Gran was clearing away the tea things and Mum was sitting at the table, chopping vegetables for dinner. They smiled as Amelia walked in, and she grinned back. Gran and Mum looked so alike. Gran's hair was short and neat, while Mum's was long like Amelia's, but they had the same laughing blue eyes.

Blue eyes like mine, thought Amelia. Dad always said she looked like Mum.

"Tell us more about your weekend," Mum said. "It sounds like you and Dad had a great time."

"It was really cool," Amelia said. "The best bit was going to the cinema. I missed Welford, though – and the kittens!"

She and her new friend Sam had

found the newborn kittens in Sam's garage, without their mother. But they had managed to find her and reunite the little family, just in time to save the tiny kittens. The cat family were now staying at Animal Ark, where the vets were looking after them until the kittens were old enough to leave their mother.

"Can I go and visit them?" asked Amelia. "I'll go to Sam's on the way and see if he wants to come too."

Gran glanced out of the window. "You won't have to do that. Here's Sam now!"

Amelia grinned. Through the window, she saw her friend and Mac, his Westie puppy, coming up the garden path.

She rushed to open the door.

Mac scrabbled at her knees, yapping happily and wagging his stubby tail. "Hi, Sam!" said Amelia. "Hello, Mac!" She knelt to stroke Mac's thick white coat and rub his pointed ears.

Sam's dark brown eyes were shining with excitement. "Hey, Amelia!" he said. "I think Mac missed you. Do you want to come and see the kittens with us?"

Amelia laughed. "Definitely! Come on – I can't wait to go to Animal Ark again!"

Outside Animal Ark, Mr Hope the vet was saying goodbye to a woman with an excitable cockapoo. The cute little dog had a plastic cone around its neck.

"Buster will need to wear it until his stitches have healed," Mr Hope was saying. When he noticed Amelia, Sam and Mac, he waved. "Hello! You must have come to see the cat family. Come on in!"

They followed Mr Hope into the surgery reception area. Amelia glanced round, thinking how strange it looked on a Sunday, with all the empty chairs and nobody sitting at the reception desk. Magazines were piled neatly on a side table, and the walls were covered in posters with information for pet owners. The one nearest the door showed two black and white rabbits. It said, "WANTED: new home for two adorable rabbit sisters!" Amelia smiled. The rabbits looked very cute.

"You can leave Mac in here," said Mr Hope, "while we're in the hotel."

"Stay, Mac," said Sam, looping the dog's lead over one of the hooks on the wall. Mac flopped down, his wagging tail thumping the floor. Sam patted his head. "Good boy!"

Mr Hope led them through to the "hotel", the cosy back room where poorly animals were kept if they needed to stay overnight. There were large, comfortable pens at floor level and smaller ones on top. In one of the bottom ones, an old, grey-muzzled dog with a bandaged leg opened one eye and closed it again.

Mrs Hope, the other vet at the surgery, was leaning over one of the pens. Her kind face lit up when she saw Amelia and Sam. "Come and look," she said.

Amelia felt excitement bubble up inside her as they peeped into the pen. Caramel, the mother cat, was lying on her side on a padded, heated cushion. She purred happily as she looked up at Amelia and Sam. Her four kittens were lying beside her, drinking her milk. Three of them were tortoiseshell, like their mother, and the fourth was ginger. Their tiny paws kneaded her soft tummy, and every now and then one gave a soft, contented squeak.

"They've grown so much since we found them," said Sam.

Amelia nodded. "Even the little ginger one." She shivered, remembering how the ginger kitten had almost died when they first found them.

"Caramel is looking after them very well," said Mrs Hope.

"How long do the kittens have to stay with her?" Sam asked.

"Until they're at least eight weeks old," Mrs Hope replied. "So about another six weeks."

Amelia and Sam shared a glance. Amelia knew he was thinking the same thing as her: *Six weeks to find all the kittens homes.* They had rescued Caramel from Mr Stevens's farm, and he had agreed to adopt her and one of the tortoiseshell kittens, who he'd named Snowdrop because of the white tip on her tail. But the other three kittens still needed owners, and Amelia was determined to find them.

And then, she thought dreamily, *maybe Mr and Mrs Hope will let me help out at*

Animal Ark all the time. The two vets had told her she wasn't old enough yet, but Amelia could think of nothing she wanted more in the whole world.

"But there's lots to do before the kittens leave Caramel," Mr Hope went on. "We need to start handling them, and playing with them every day. They have to learn to be comfortable around people while they're tiny. Then they'll become good pets."

Read **Bunny Trouble** to find out what happens next ...

Animal Advice

Do you love animals as much as Amelia and Sam? Here are some tips on how to look after them from veterinary surgeon Sarah McGurk.

Caring for your pet

1. Animals need clean water at all times.
2. They need to be fed too – ask your vet what kind of food is best, and how much the animal needs.
3. Some animals, such as dogs, need exercise every day.
4. Animals also need lots of love. You should always be very gentle with your pets and be careful not to do anything that might hurt them.

When to go to the vet

metimes animals get ill. Like you, they will mostly get

etter on their own. But if your pet has hurt itself or

ems very unwell, then a trip to the vet might be needed.

me pets also need to be vaccinated, to prevent them

m getting dangerous diseases. Your vet can tell you

at your pet needs.

Helping wildlife

Always ask an adult before you go near any animals

you don't know.

If you find an animal or bird which is injured or can't

move, it is best not to touch it.

If you are worried, you can phone an animal charity

such as the RSPCA (SSPCA in Scotland) for help.

Where animals need you!

Kitten Rescue
Lucy Daniels

Bunny Trouble
Lucy Daniels

Fox Cub Danger
Lucy Daniels

Puppy in Peril
Lucy Daniels

The Purrfect Sleepover
Lucy Daniels

Doggy Drama
Lucy Daniels

Runaway Hamster
Lucy Daniels

Guinea Pig Superstar
Lucy Daniels

The Lonely Pony
Lucy Daniels

Scaredy-Dog
Lucy Daniels

Lost Kitten
Lucy Daniels

Llama on the Loose
Lucy Daniels

Reindeer Recovery
Lucy Daniels

The Magic Bunny
Lucy Daniels

www.animalark.co.uk